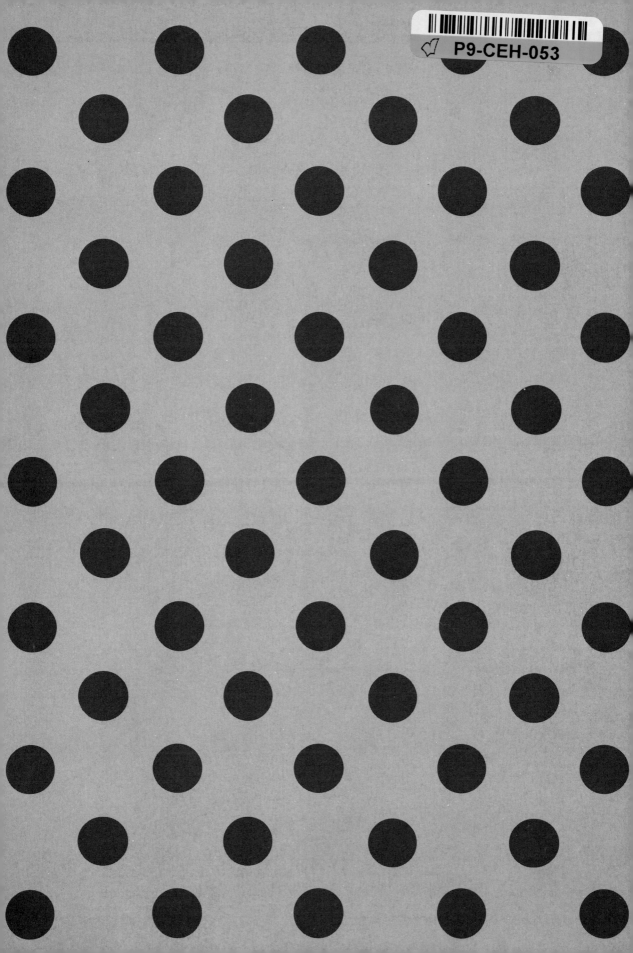

Produced by Kroha Associates, Inc.
Middletown, Connecticut.

Printed in the United States of America.

ISBN 1-56326-100-6

Disney Books By Mail offers a selection of entertaining
audio and video programs. For more information, write:
Disney Books By Mail, P.O. Box 11440, Des Moines, Iowa 50336

Daisy's Birthday Party

By Ruth Lerner Perle

One morning, Minnie looked at the big calendar on her wall. "Hooray!" she cried. "Tomorrow is Daisy's birthday party!" Minnie thought of the games and presents and goodies that would be at the party, but most of all she was thinking of how to make this the happiest birthday Daisy would ever have.

Minnie took her blue party dress with the pretty ruffles out of the closet. She held it up under her chin and looked in the mirror.

Then she took her Mary Janes out of their box and made sure they were nice and shiny.

Minnie laid all her clothes out carefully so that they would be ready for the next morning.

"Now," she thought, "I'd better get a wonderful present for Daisy — something that will really make her happy."
Minnie took her change purse and hurried off.

Minnie's first stop was at the toy store. She looked at stuffed animals, dolls, games, balls, and jump ropes. They were nice, but they were not special enough.

"Daisy already has lots of toys," Minnie said.

Next, Minnie went to the book store. She looked at picture books and pop-up books and read-along books and videotapes. But nothing seemed right.

Then Minnie went to the drugstore. She saw pretty
soaps and sachets and bubble bath. Then, out of the
corner of her eye, Minnie saw the perfect gift!

There, at the next counter, Minnie saw the most beautiful bow. It was bright yellow with big white hearts all over it.

"That bow will go perfectly with Daisy's yellow party dress," Minnie said to herself. "It is the perfect gift for her. No one else would think of giving Daisy something like this."

When Minnie took the yellow bow off the display case, she saw another bow right next to it. It was sky blue with white hearts, just like her own party dress.

"Ooh," Minnie whispered. "If I wear that bow, Daisy and I will look just like sisters!"

When Minnie came home, she wrapped Daisy's yellow bow in green tissue paper and tied the package with shiny pink ribbon. Then she took out her crayons and her silver sparkles and made a birthday card.

On the day of the party, Minnie took a nice long bath to make sure she was squeaky clean. She put on her party dress and shiny shoes and, as a finishing touch, she put her beautiful blue bow on her head. Minnie looked in the mirror. *Very pretty*, she thought to herself.

When she was all ready, Minnie picked up Daisy's gift. She liked the way the present looked with its pretty bow on top.

There were lots of guests at Daisy's party. There were Penny, Clarabelle, Lilly, and some other girls Minnie didn't know. Everybody had brought presents and piled them up around the couch.

Daisy gave each of her friends a hug. "Thank you! Thank you!" she said. "After we have cake and ice cream, I'll open all these beautiful presents. I can hardly wait!"

Everyone sat down at the table. They had ice cream with strawberry sauce, lemonade, and chocolate chip cookies.

It was time for birthday cake! Everybody clapped and sang Happy Birthday to Daisy. Daisy closed her eyes and made a wish. She took a deep breath and blew out all the candles.

Daisy cut the cake. She smiled at Minnie and gave her the first piece. "You look pretty in that bow," Daisy said. "I wish I had a bow like that."

Minnie just smiled, and started to eat her cake.

Soon it was time to open the birthday presents. Everybody followed Daisy to the living room and gathered around her on the sofa.

Daisy opened her first present. It was a wooly blue sweater from her Great Aunt Dora.

"My aunt knits the best sweaters!" Daisy said.

"It's exactly the same color as Minnie's dress!" Penny said.

Next Daisy unwrapped Clarabelle's present.
It was exactly the same bow that Minnie had bought for Daisy.
"Oh, thank you so much, Clarabelle!" Daisy said. "This is a perfect gift. It's exactly the right color for my dress!" Daisy gave Clarabelle a hug.
Minnie felt her heart pound. She tried her best not to cry, but a tear welled in the corner of her eye.

Daisy started to unwrap Minnie's gift next.

"I can't wait to see what Minnie brought me. I know it will be special," Daisy said, smiling at her friend.

She untied the ribbon and took off the tissue paper.

"It's another yellow bow!" Daisy said. "It's the same bow Clarabelle gave me!"

"Now you have two bows to go with your yellow party dress," Penny said. "But you don't have any bow to go with your new blue sweater."

"Too bad," said Clarabelle.

That gave Minnie an idea.

She stood up on a chair and said, "Listen everybody! I have a special magic trick in honor of Daisy's birthday. But everybody must close their eyes — and no peeking!"

While no one was looking, Minnie took the yellow bow out of Daisy's hand and replaced it with her own blue one.

Then she said, "Abracadabra! Five, four, three, two! The yellow bow is now bright blue!"

Everybody opened their eyes. There was a sky blue bow in Daisy's hands.

"What a wonderful trick!" everybody shouted, clapping their hands.
"What a birthday surprise!" cried Lilly.
"I must admit that was clever," Clarabelle added.
"That bow is just perfect for your new sweater!" Penny said.

Daisy ran over to Minnie and gave her a great big kiss.
"Oh, Minnie!" she said. "You're the smartest, funniest friend anyone could wish for. I'll keep this bow forever and ever. It will remind me of your magical birthday trick and what a wonderful friend you are!"

Daisy sure loved that blue bow! Birthday surprises are the best surprises of all!

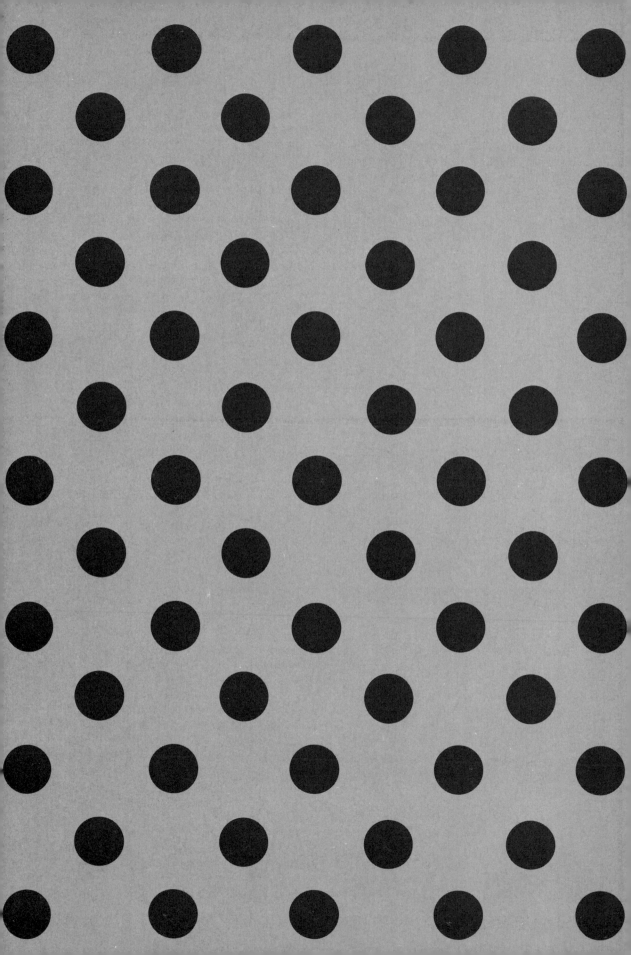